The Little MERMAID

AND OTHER FISHY TALES

Written and Illustrated by

JANE RAY

BOXER BOOKS

With grateful thanks to Ann Jungman
for her expertise and help in researching these stories with me.
Jane Ray

First published in North America in 2014 by Boxer Books Limited.
First published in Great Britain in 2014
by Boxer Books Limited.
www.boxerbooks.com

Library of Congress Cataloging-in-Publication Data available.

The illustrations were prepared using Scraperboard, where the line is etched
onto a thin layer of white china clay on board coated with black India ink.

The text is set in Garamond.

ISBN 978-1-907967-81-8

1 3 5 7 9 10 8 6 4 2

Printed in China

All of our papers are sourced from
managed forests and renewable resources.

For Gill Wild

CONTENTS

INTRODUCTION

I have always loved stories – stories that my grandma told me, little fragments of stories I've overheard in cafes or on the train (I'm very nosy!), as well as stories that I've made up or that have arrived in my head as dreams.

There is nothing as intriguing as a good story. The best ones creep into the imagination and linger there, surfacing when you least expect them. Ghost stories, adventure stories, funny stories, fairytales and folktales – I try to remember them all, to keep them alive.

Of course, the best way to keep a story alive is to tell it, again and again, to different people and in different ways. And the truly wonderful thing about a story is that you can change it and make it yours. Every time you tell a story you breathe new life into it and you pass it on to someone else for safe keeping.

That is what I'm doing here, in this book, my second collection of stories for you. The first one was all about birds – *The Emperor's Nightingale and Other Feathery Tales*. This one, as you have probably guessed from the title, is about fish and the sea.

People are always drawn to the sea and I

am no exception. I love it in all its moods and seasons. I love the mesmerizing lapping of calm summer waves and the spectacular crashing of stormy breakers. I love the sound it makes after it has hit the shore and rolls back with a rush of clattering, shushing stones. I love the sight of a silver path across a calm sea when the moon is full.

The sea is full of mystery and danger – and full of life, both real and imagined. It is hardly surprising that it has cast up so many stories over the centuries. Sailors and fishermen have always been at the mercy of the sea, living dangerous and exciting lives.

They are often the heroes and tellers of these stories, inventing tales of mermaids and gods and monsters to make sense of the dangers they face, and creating a culture of their own.

Under the sea there is a whole other world, with its own plants and animals: a world in which we, as humans, can't survive without using cumbersome breathing equipment. The real animals and fish that live there are as extraordinary as the invented ones. For a long time, as a child, I thought that the octopus was a mythical creature – surely nothing as bizarre as an eight-limbed huge-headed monster with suckers and tentacles could really exist?

Life on earth is reflected under the sea. Shoals of fish like flocks of birds mass together and turn suddenly at an unseen signal. Seaweed and anemones and coral echo the plant life on earth. Turtles and seals, otters and great walruses are the animals of the ocean, and surely the massive blue whale is an aquatic dinosaur?

I've thrown my net as wide as I could to bring you these fishy tales. From Africa to Orkney, from Greece to Greenland, there are stories here as ancient as a grain of sand and, in the wonderful poem "Whalesong" by Sophie Stephenson-Wright, as contemporary as today's news. Each one is a pearl.

I hope you enjoy reading them as much as I have enjoyed telling them.

THE KINGDOM
UNDER THE SEA

This story is very famous in Japan. In a tale of transformations, time tricks, and turtles, we journey to an underwater kingdom of great beauty and also travel through the centuries.

I always think there is something mysterious about turtles. They lay their eggs on the beach by moonlight and return with their newly hatched young to the water when the tide turns. It seems quite fitting that they should be capable of transforming themselves completely.

Urashima Taro was a young fisherman who lived on a Japanese island long ago. Every day he took his boat out to sea and fished patiently, hour after hour.

Every evening he hauled the boat up the beach and took his fish to the market to sell, always keeping one back to share with his mother for supper. They would eat together, watching the sun set over the sea, and tell each other how lucky they were.

One evening on his way home,
Taro came upon a group of small boys
standing around a turtle lying helpless
on its back. Every time the poor creature
tried to right itself, the boys pushed it
over again, laughing at its plight and
poking it with sticks.

"Why are you tormenting an innocent
creature? How could you be so cruel?"
Taro shouted at the boys. He chased
them away and gently lifted the turtle,
turning her the right way up. Then he
carefully brushed the sand from her shell
and carried her down to the sea. "Go
back to your family, Venerable Turtle,"
he said, "and may you live for
a thousand years!"

Taro continued on his journey home and after cooking the fish, he and his mother sat talking late into the night.

The next day dawned fair and bright and Taro once again sat in his boat, rocking gently on the calm sea. Quite suddenly he heard a voice calling his name. "Taro, Taro." He turned around, looking this way and that, until he realized that the voice was coming from the water. He looked down and there was a turtle, swimming alongside the boat.

This is very strange, thought Taro to himself. *Turtles are usually so shy — I hardly ever see them and now I see two in two days!* To the turtle he said, "I rescued one of your kind just yesterday! What can I do for you today?"

But the turtle answered, "I have come to do something for you, my friend! My master is the Dragon King, who lives in his glorious kingdom under the sea. He has sent me to bring you to him because he wishes to express his gratitude for your help and kindness."

"I am very honored, turtle," said Taro, "but I cannot survive under the sea — I would drown."

"Not in my care," said the Turtle.

"I will give you magical powers."

It would be a fine thing to see the
Kingdom under the Sea – how could
Taro resist such an invitation? He
clambered out of his boat and onto
the turtle's back.

They sped off, plunging down into
the ocean. Taro found he could indeed
breathe in the water, and he looked in

amazement at the beauty all around
him. They passed through great shoals
of tiny glinting fish. There were jellyfish
and dolphins, and an octopus drifted
by. Tendrils of green seaweed brushed at
Taro's legs and looking down he saw a
sea garden of exquisite anemones.

Eventually they arrived at the gates of
a beautiful palace. The turtle set
Taro down and he walked through
the gates into a courtyard paved with

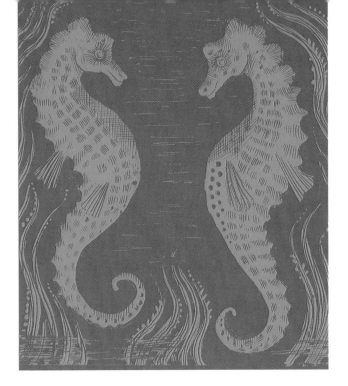

mother-of-pearl. He was greeted by a couple of sea horses who led him through to the throne room. There, seated on a magnificent coral throne, was the Dragon King himself. And at his side was the most beautiful girl Taro had ever seen.

"Is this the man who saved you yesterday?" the Dragon King asked the girl.

"Oh yes, Father – that's him," said the girl. Taro was bewildered. "I was the little turtle you rescued yesterday," the girl explained. "I sent my servant to fetch you so that we could thank you properly."

"There is no need," said Taro, bowing low to the girl.

But the Dragon King thundered, "There is every need – you saved my daughter's life and you are a hero! She wishes to marry you and have you live here with us under the ocean. What do you say?"

Taro looked at the lovely princess, with her flowing black hair and kimono of turquoise silk, and said yes!

Immediately the marriage celebrations began. The wedding lasted for three days and three nights, with dancing and feasting and great rejoicing throughout the Kingdom under the Sea. It was a magical place, where youth was not touched by time and happiness always reigned.

Surrounding the coral palace was a wonderful garden where all four seasons existed at once.

In one corner the cherry
blossom drifted down to
the grass.

In another the flowers bloomed with all
the glory of full summer.

A third corner was ablaze
with crimson maples,

and in the fourth the bamboo sparkled with frost.

Taro and his lovely bride wandered hand in hand, completely happy. Quite suddenly, he thought to himself, *How my mother would love this place!* As soon as he started thinking about her he realized how worried she must be. He hadn't been home for three days and three nights. She would have had no fish for supper. She would think he had drowned!

"I must go home, just for a while, and tell my mother I am safe and happy," he said to his princess.

Although she was sad to let him go, she knew that he must. If he loved his mother as she loved her father, there would be no stopping him.

So the princess summoned the large turtle to take Taro home. Before he left, she gave him a mysterious red-lacquered box tied with a cord of scarlet silk.

"Promise me you will keep this box with you always, but that you will never open it?" she said.

Taro promised and kissing her, he climbed onto the turtle's back.

Swiftly they sped back along the ocean floor and then climbed up, up to the surface. Once on shore, Taro made his way toward his mother's house. He was surprised to see some new houses along the beach, and farther on a new harbor. As he walked, he became more and more confused. The people he passed in the street were all strangers and none of the buildings looked the same. He was filled with fear and stumbled on, desperately trying to find something familiar.

At last he recognized the stream and the stepping stones in the garden where his mother's house had stood. But the house itself was different and when he knocked on the door it was opened by a stranger. "I am Urashima Taro – where is my mother?" he asked.

"This is my house," answered the stranger. "The only Urashima Taro I know of drowned three hundred years ago, according to legend, and his mother died not long after of a broken heart."

Taro staggered away toward the sea, reeling with shock and grief, not knowing what to do or where to go. He fell to his knees in the sand and the

red-lacquered box fell from the sleeve
of his kimono. He tugged at the silken
cord, thinking the box might take him
back to his wife. The box fell open and
out came a soft wisp of smoke. It curled
around him and, as he looked inside, he
saw that his hands were the hands of an
old man.

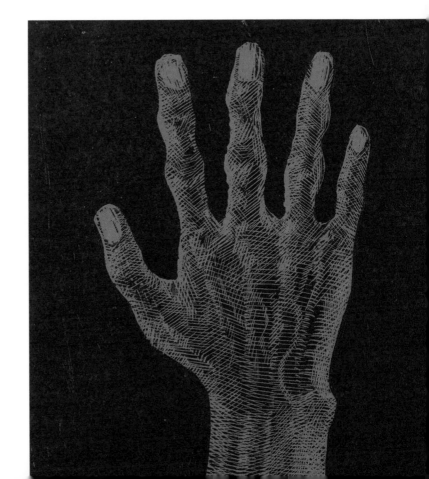

He tried to get up from his knees, to find a rock pool to see his reflection, but his joints were weak and his head pounded. The waves crashing on the shore carried the sound of the princess's voice to his ears.

"Taro, oh my love," – he could just make out what she was saying – "I told you not to open the box. It holds your old age and your death ..."

As the light seeped from the sky and the gulls wheeled overhead, the figure of an ancient man lay lifeless on the beach.

THE LOBSTER QUADRILLE

This wonderful piece of nonsense comes from Alice's Adventures in Wonderland where, in the logic of dreams, Alice finds herself on the seashore in deep conversation with a Mock Turtle and a Gryphon and is treated to a performance of their dance.

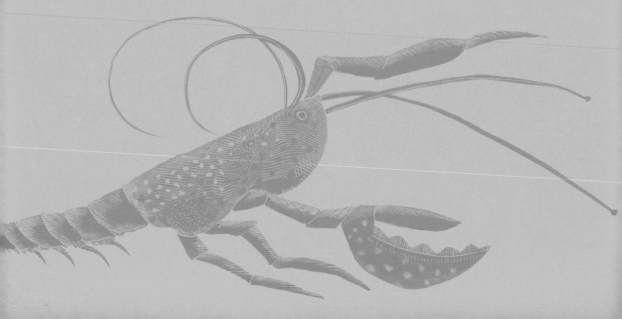

Will you walk a little faster?"
said a whiting to a snail.
"There's a porpoise close behind us,
and he's treading on my tail.
See how eagerly the lobsters and the
turtles all advance!

They are waiting on the shingle – will you
come and join the dance?
Will you, won't you, will you, won't you,
will you join the dance?
Will you, won't you, will you, won't you,
won't you join the dance?

"You can really have no notion how
delightful it will be.
When they take us up and throw us,
with the lobsters, out to sea!"

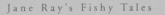

But the snail replied "Too far, too far!" and
gave a look askance –
Said he thanked the whiting kindly,
but he would not join the dance.

Would not, could not, would not,
could not, would not join the dance.
Would not, could not, would not, could not,
could not join the dance.

"What
matters it
how far we
go?" his scaly
friend replied.
"There is another
shore, you know,
upon the other side.
The further off
from England
the nearer is to France –
Then turn not pale,
beloved snail,
but come and join the dance.
Will you, won't you, will you,
won't you, will you join the dance?

Will you, won't you, will you, won't you,
won't you join the dance?"

– Lewis Carroll

THE LITTLE MERMAID

This story was originally written as a ballet by Hans Christian Andersen in 1836. It has been retold and reshaped many times, the most famous version probably being the Disney film. The story of the conflict between the two different cultures above and below the waves, and a young woman's determination to go her own way, is universal and timeless. I have changed the ending of the story because the original is very much of its time, with attitudes toward women that are hard to make sense of today.

Far out to sea, and deeper down
than you can imagine, is a place of
great beauty and mystery. Light filters
through the blue waters, casting strange
ripples on the seabed, and colorful fish
swim in gardens of branching coral
and flowing seaweed.

This is where the merfolk lived long ago, ruled over by the Sea King. His castle lay in the deepest part of the ocean and was made of seashells and mother-of-pearl that gleamed in the dappled half light.

The Sea King had a daughter, a mermaid, who was quick and clever. He loved her more than anything in his vast kingdom and her happiness was all that mattered to him. She was full of curiosity about what lay around and above her. At night she looked up through the dark blue water and could just make out the stars and the pale moon glimmering in the sky. She had heard many stories of the human

world – of ships and cities, of men and women, of green woods, perfumed flowers, and feathered birds that flew and sang.

The Little Mermaid longed to go there and see for herself. "I want to see the world above the waves, Father. Let me go and explore? Please?"

"But our world is far more wonderful – why do you want to see above? It is dry and gray up there – and no one has a tail," he said. But even as he answered, he remembered his own youthful longing to see above the waves, and so with many warnings, the Sea King let his precious daughter go.

The sun had just set as the Little
Mermaid raised her head above the surface
of the waves. The air felt wonderfully
fresh and the sea was very calm.

Ahead of her lay a ship with three masts and sails of strong canvas. From the deck came the sound of music and laughter and the Little Mermaid saw finely dressed people dancing together, on feet and legs. They all looked so beautiful in the soft candlelight, but her eye was caught by the most beautiful of all – a young prince, with dark curls and laughing eyes. The Little Mermaid could hardly take her eyes from his face and even though the night became darker and colder, with a rising wind that ruffled the water, she was warmed through with love.

But a storm was brewing. Lightning

struck and the wind filled the sails and
whipped the waves until they were the size
of mountains. The ship rolled and creaked
and the mainmast snapped like a reed.
The ship began to keel over on its side.

The Little Mermaid watched
horrified, as the sailors and the young
prince struggled to right the ship. They
tried their best, but suddenly, with a
terrible creaking groan, the great ship
split in two and the Little Mermaid
watched as the men and women fell
into the sea.

Their feet and legs were little use to
them in the water and many people
were lost.

The Little Mermaid dived beneath
the waves. At first she thought she could
save the prince by taking him down
to her father's kingdom, but then she
remembered that he couldn't survive
under water. Her search for him became
more frantic. She looked everywhere,
diving and surfacing again and again,
until at last she found him, struggling
to stay afloat and tiring fast. She took
him in her arms and let the waves carry
them, until the storm began to blow
itself out.

The first light of dawn rose on a calm
sea. The Little Mermaid began to swim
toward the shore, the young prince still
unconscious in her arms. As she swam
closer, she could see how beautiful the
land was, with snow-capped mountains,
dark forests, and green pastures that
flowed down to the sea. She swam into
a shallow cove and laid the young prince
down in the warm morning sun. She
waited out of sight in the water and
watched over him until rescue came.

Before long, a young woman walking
along the beach saw the prince lying on
the sand. She ran to him, and kneeling
beside him called to some distant
fishermen for help. The prince woke up

then, and smiling up into the eyes of the young woman, he thanked her again and again, for he thought it was she who had saved him from the stormy waters.

The Little Mermaid watched as the prince was helped home and then she swam sadly away.

Back in her father's kingdom under the waves, she pined for the prince and the wonderful things she had glimpsed in his world. She would often visit the beach, just to gaze at the little cove where she had left him, hoping that he might walk past.

She told no one. She had no appetite. She could not sleep. She began to imagine a life on land, a life with him,

with two legs instead of a tail. Unable to
bear her longing any more she decided
to visit the ancient Sea Witch.

The Sea Witch lived in the darkest,
bleakest part of the ocean, beyond the
walls of the kingdom. Everyone was
afraid of her, but she was powerful and
full of magic and the Little Mermaid
knew that no one else could help her.

The Little Mermaid had never
ventured into this part of the seabed

before. It
was murky
and the
water
churned in
whirlpools.

Long slimy ropes of seaweed reached out to ensnare her as she passed and sea snakes lurked in the gloom. Here lay the skeletons of drowned sailors and the barnacled remains of shipwrecks. Only the thought of the prince gave her the courage to go on.

In a terrible hovel made of bones sat the Sea Witch, draped in tattered garments stolen from the drowned, feeding the writhing sea serpents that clustered around her.

"I know what you have come for!" she cackled, as the Little Mermaid cowered in the shadows. "You want to swap your tail for legs because you've fallen in love with a human. You are a fool! But it will please me to do this.

I will enjoy watching your dreams
shattered. I will give you a potion.
When you drink it, your tail will wither
away and in its place will be bony legs
and little feet. But there is a price, my
girl. Are you willing to pay?"

"I will pay whatever you ask," said
the Little Mermaid. Her fear somehow
made her even more determined.
"What is your price?"

"I will take your voice," said the
Sea Witch.

The Little Mermaid hesitated for a
moment. She closed her eyes and saw
the prince once again in her mind's eye,
remembering how it felt to hold him
in her arms.

"I will pay," she said.

The Sea Witch began to stir a bubbling cauldron of thick black liquid. She growled and moaned as she stirred, adding shells full of mysterious ingredients.

When she was done she handed the Little Mermaid a tiny glass bottle. And then, suddenly, the Sea Witch loomed toward the Little Mermaid and kissed her. The Little Mermaid tried to cry out but there was no sound, no sound at all. The evil Sea Witch had extracted her price.

With the potion clasped in her hand the Little Mermaid swam from the Sea Witch's lair as fast as she possibly could.

She passed the coral walls of her father's kingdom and realized with a wave of grief that she could not explain or say goodbye. There was no going back.

The sun was just rising when she emerged from the water. She drank the foul potion in one gulp and when she reached the shoreline, she found to her amazement that she could walk out of the sea and up the beach on strong, straight legs. The pebbles and stones were sharp on her feet and she gasped with pain.

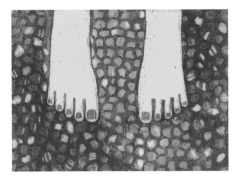

The prince was out walking by the ocean and as soon as he saw the poor young woman he ran toward her. Wrapping her in his cloak, he took her into the warmth and safety of the palace. There the Little Mermaid was looked after, for it was the custom in his country to take in any traveler and treat them as an honored guest.

And so it was that she was bathed and fed and given a soft bed to sleep in until she began to recover her strength.

The prince was very drawn to this beautiful and silent stranger and spent hours in her company. The Little Mermaid was so enraptured by him that she was able to push away her thoughts of home. Even though she could not speak there was an understanding between them that transcended words. They laughed together, listened to music, and watched the sea and the sky. Their friendship grew stronger each day.

Then one morning, the prince told the Little Mermaid of his recent shipwreck and of his rescue by a young

woman on the beach. It was agony for
the Little Mermaid not to be able to tell
him that it was she who had rescued him
and not the other girl. But worse was
to come.

"I am to be married to her," he said.
"The young woman who was my rescuer
is the princess of a neighboring kingdom
and everyone approves of the match."

Even through her own tears the Little
Mermaid could see that the prince didn't
look very happy. "It is my duty," he
said, "but what is truly strange is that
even though she can speak, I don't have
the conversations with her that I do
with you." The young prince sighed
and kicked at the pebbles at his feet.

The marriage drew closer. The cooks worked tirelessly preparing the magnificent wedding feast. Tailors and seamstresses stitched through the night to finish the wedding garments. Musicians rehearsed glorious music for the ball that would celebrate the joining of the young prince and princess.

On the night before the
wedding the Little
Mermaid and
the prince walked
together along the cliffs
above the beach. The sun
was setting and the waves
rolled and crashed onto the shingle
below them. The Little Mermaid was
weighed down with grief at the prospect
of losing the man that she loved so
much. The prince knew that he had
fallen so deeply in love with his
strange silent companion that he
could not marry the princess in
the morning.

No one is quite sure what happened next, but a group of fishermen hauling their boat in say that there was a sudden squally gust of wind and they saw two figures fall from the cliff and into the froth of the waves.

The men rowed as hard as they could to try and rescue whoever had fallen, but there was no sign of anyone in the water – just two great white birds circling up from the waves and flying into the crimson sunset.

THE FISHERMAN
AND HIS WIFE

This story appears in many different cultures – Chinese and Russian to name but two. This version comes from a treasury of fairy stories called The Juniper Tree, *collected by The Grimm Brothers.*

I feel sure the reason it is so widespread is because societies the world over recognize that very human tendency to always want a bit more.

Once upon a time there was a
fisherman and his wife who were so
very poor that they lived under a rusty
bucket on the seashore. Every day the
fisherman would row out to sea, drop
his nets over the side of the boat, and sit
all day on the rocking waves. Some days
he would catch a tiny little tiddler, some
days his nets were full, and some days he
caught absolutely nothing.

One day he was sitting in his boat,
when suddenly he felt a tugging and a
pulling. There in his
net was a beautiful
big silver fish with
rainbows in its scales,
gleaming in the
sunlight.

The fisherman was astonished at his
luck – but he was even more amazed
when the fish spoke to him!

"Please, Fisherman, don't eat me. Put me back in the water and let me swim free."

"I wouldn't dream of doing anything else," said the fisherman. "A fish that can talk is a rare thing indeed – I don't want to eat you!"

He untangled the fish from the net and gently placed it back in the clear water. It swam swiftly to the bottom, calling out as it went, "Thank you, Fisherman. If you ever need me just call my name – I am the King of Fishes!"

Well, how lucky is that? thought the fisherman. He bundled up his nets, rowed to shore, and ran up the beach to his wife.

"Didn't you catch anything today?" she asked.

"Well," said the man, "I did catch the King of Fishes, but he was far too beautiful to eat so I let him go."

"And you didn't ask for anything in return?" said the woman, exasperated.

"Well no," said the man. "I didn't think of that. It was enough just to see such a beautiful creature. What should I have asked for?"

"You could've asked for a little cottage for us to live in, with a garden and smoke curling from the chimney, instead of this rusty old bucket that lets the rain in. A fish like that is a magical thing! He could grant you any wish you could think of! You let him go free, gave him his life – surely he will give you something in return? You must go straight back and ask."

The fisherman thought his wife had a point, so he went back to the shoreline and rowed out across the blue-green sea, calling softly to the King of Fishes.

Almost at once, the King of Fishes was

swimming alongside the little wooden boat.

"How can I help you, Fisherman?" he asked.

"Well," said the fisherman, "I'm sorry to bother you, but my wife thought you might be willing to grant us a wish."

"And what does she want?" asked the fish.

"A little cottage," said the fisherman, "with a garden and smoke curling from the chimney, instead of the rusty bucket we live under now."

"Look to the shoreline," said the

King of Fishes, and he sank beneath the greeny waters.

The fisherman looked to the shore, and there it was – the prettiest little cottage you could imagine, with a thatched roof, a garden all around, and smoke curling from the chimney pot.

He rowed back to his wife and together they walked around their new

home. A fire burned brightly in the
kitchen grate and a clock ticked on the
mantelpiece.

In the bedroom there were soft pillows
on the bed and a warm quilt. The garden
was full of flowers and vegetables, and
hens scratched under the fruit trees.

"This is perfect," said the fisherman.
"We shall be very happy."

And they were – for a week or two.
But after a while the woman said to her

husband, "I just wish you had asked King Fish for something a little bigger. We could do with a few more rooms really, and then of course we'd need servants, and a garden big enough for a fountain ..."

So the fisherman rowed slowly off, across a gray and choppy sea.

He sighed and called softly to the King of Fishes.

The great silver fish rose through the swirling water. "What do you want now, Fisherman?" he asked.

"I'm sorry, but my wife wants more space. She wants a bigger house, and she also wants servants, and a garden with room for a fountain.

"And she says a carriage would be nice, with four white horses. Oh, and a flagpole on the roof ..."

"Look to the shoreline," said the King of Fishes, and he plunged down into the water.

The fisherman turned his little boat around and there, on the edge of the sand, was the finest house he had ever seen.

The fisherman's wife was delighted. She spent her days wandering around the fine rooms and gardens, giving orders to the servants, and riding out in her carriage. But one evening, as the couple sat by the grand marble fireplace, the woman turned to her husband.

"This is all very fine," she said, "but

what I'd really like is a castle – a proper
castle with a moat and a drawbridge.
Actually, I'd like to be King! Go back
and ask the fish to make me KING!!"

The fisherman was aghast. "But my dear wife," he said, "we have everything we could possibly ever need. Why do you want more?" But his wife went on and on at him until, in the end, he found himself rowing out to sea in stormy waters, calling softly to the King of Fishes.

The great fish rose again from the waves. "And what now?" he asked.

The fisherman, head bowed, mumbled that his wife wanted a castle now, and worse, she wanted to be King.

"Look to the shoreline," said the fish sadly. "It is as she wishes." And he sank once more beneath the waves.

When the fisherman got back to land, there stood the most magnificent castle. The fisherman walked across the drawbridge and into a great marble hall, all hung with tapestries. At the far end of the hall sat his wife on a silver throne. She was surrounded by courtiers and ladies-in-waiting and guardsmen and servants, all doing as she commanded.

But as the weeks and months went by, the woman got a little bored with just ruling the country. What she really wanted was to make the sun and the moon rise, to cause the wind to blow and the tides to turn.

"I want to be God," she said.

"No," said the fisherman, "I'm not asking the King of Fishes for that. How ridiculous."

But the fisherman's wife said, "I command you to go and ask that big fish to make me God. I am your king and you are my subject. You must do as I say!"

With grief and shame in his heart, the fisherman climbed into his boat.

The waves were pitching and boiling,
dark and treacherous. Out at sea, he
called once more to the King of Fishes.

Once again the great silver fish
emerged from the heaving ocean.

"What more can she possibly want,
this wife of yours?" he asked.

The fisherman could hardly bring
himself to speak. He mumbled under his
breath. But the King of Fishes couldn't
hear him over the roar of the storm and
the fisherman had to shout at the top of
his voice, "My wife wants to be God!"

Everything stopped. The wind
dropped, the rain ceased, the waves
stilled. The King of Fishes looked sadly
at the fisherman.

"Look to the shoreline," he said, and
in a flash of silver and rainbows, he
dived beneath the waves.

And sitting bobbing in his little boat, the fisherman looked back to the shoreline, where he could just make out the figure of his wife sitting on the edge of an upturned rusty bucket.

A BALLAD OF JOHN SILVER

This fabulous poem by John Masefield has a lovely rolling rhythm and a real sense of the wild and gruesome life that pirates in the eighteenth century must have lived. You can almost feel the barnacles and smell the salt and the gunpowder!

We were schooner-rigged and rakish,

With a long and lissom hull,

And we flew the pretty colours of

the crossbones and the skull;

We'd a big black Jolly Roger

flapping grimly at the fore,

And we sailed the Spanish Water

in the happy days of yore.

We'd a long brass gun amidships,
like a well-conducted ship,
We had each a brace of pistols
and a cutlass at the hip;
It's a point which tells against us,
and a fact to be deplored,
But we chased the goodly merchant-men
and laid their ships aboard.

Then the dead men fouled the scuppers
and the wounded filled the chains,
And the paint-work was all spatter-
dashed with other people's brains,
She was boarded, she was looted,
she was scuttled till she sank.
And the pale survivors left us
by the medium of the plank.

O! Then it was (while standing by
the taffrail on the poop)
We could hear the drowning
folk lament the absent chicken
coop;*
Then, having washed the
blood away, we'd little
else to do
Than to dance a quiet
hornpipe as the old
salts taught us to.

O! The fiddle
on the fo'c'sle,
and the slapping
naked soles
And the genial "Down

the middle, Jake,

and curtsey when she rolls!"

With the silver seas around us

and the pale moon overhead,

And the look-out not a-looking

and his pipe bowl glowing red.

Ah! The pig-tailed, quidding pirates

and the pretty pranks we played,

All have since been put a stop-to

by the naughty Board of Trade;

The schooners and the merry crews

are laid away to rest,

A little south the sunset in the islands

of the Blest.

— John Masefield

*   *Chicken coop — this is slang for a cage
or prison cell for the pirates' captives. It was
preferable to being thrown overboard or
walking the plank.*

MONKEY AND SHARK

This African story is a "trickster tale," a form very common in folk tales, where one creature outwits another. In these stories, there is always a feeling of sympathy for the "little guy," who uses brains and cunning to trick the stronger, more powerful creature.

Right on the very edge of Africa, where the jungle meets the sea, there are mangrove swamps. Here, monkeys call to one another across the treetops, feasting on the delicious fruit and swinging from branch to branch.

In this wonderful place there was
once a group of monkeys, who loved
to drop fruit on a school of sharks who
swam near the swamp below. This had
kept them amused for years, because
it made the sharks very cross. But, of
course, the sharks couldn't catch the
monkeys sitting in the treetops.

But there was one shark who enjoyed eating the fruit so much, he turned up every day. One day Shark said to Monkey,

"Thank you so much for all this beautiful fruit you give me – I do so enjoy it. The other sharks think me very odd, but I love it!"

"Think nothing of it," said Monkey. "There is more fruit here than we can possibly eat and you are most welcome to it."

This went on from month to month, until one day Shark turned up looking troubled. "What's the matter?" asked Monkey.

"Well," said Shark, "it seems unfair that you keep giving me this delicious fruit and yet I never give you anything in return."

"There's nothing else I need," said Monkey. "I certainly don't fancy any of your smelly old fish!"

"So is there really nothing that I can give to you?" persisted Shark.

"No – not really," said Monkey. "Please don't worry yourself."

But all of a sudden the shark stuck his head out of the water.

"I know what you'd like," he said. "It's so very hot in the jungle – why

don't I take you for a ride on my back,
out across the beautiful cool ocean?"

Well Monkey had often wondered
what it would be like out on the
beautiful blue ocean so she agreed and
jumped onto Shark's back. Suddenly
the air was filled with the screams and
chattering of the other monkeys. "Don't
go," they cried. "Don't you know you
can never trust a shark?"

But it was too late. Shark skimmed through the blue water, with Monkey hanging on tight to his fin. It was indeed cool and refreshing but Monkey wasn't at all happy.

"Dear friend Shark," she shouted, above the roar and rush of the water, "thank you very much, but I'd like to go back now, please."

"Sorry, Monkey," called Shark, "I'm afraid I have other plans for you. The King of the Sharks is sick and only a fine monkey heart will cure him."

Monkey thought quickly. "A monkey heart, you say. Oh, now why didn't you tell me this earlier? I'm afraid to say that monkeys never take their hearts when they go traveling."

"You mean to tell me," said Shark, "that you don't have it with you? Well where is it?"

"I keep it in a hole in the big mangrove tree," said Monkey. "Just turn around and take me back, and I can pick it up quick as quick. Hurry, my dear Shark friend – if the King is ill we mustn't waste a moment!"

Shark turned around and swam as fast as he could back to the mangrove swamp.

"Which tree is your heart in?" asked Shark.

"The big one, there, with the branch hanging down to the water. Swim past it as close as you can."

Shark swam close to the branch and

Monkey grabbed it
and raced to the top
of the tree.

"Have you found it,
Monkey?" called Shark
from the water
far below.

"Oh, my dear friend Shark," called
down Monkey, "I was a fool to believe a
shark could be my friend, but not as big
a fool as you. Where else could my heart
possibly be, but beating in my chest?"

The treetops rang with the laughter
of the monkeys as they pelted the shark
below with fruit.

ARION AND THE DOLPHIN

An extraordinary relationship has always existed between humans and dolphins. There are many incidents of dolphins coming to the rescue of people in trouble, and numerous stories of friendship and trust. Their expressions suggest smiles, and they have an intelligence and sensitivity that appeals to humankind. But sadly, human behavior, through overfishing and pollution, threatens the very survival of these beautiful creatures.

This story, based on an ancient Greek legend, illustrates both aspects of this relationship.

There was once a young musician called Arion who lived at the court of King Periander of Corinth, in Greece. The sound of his singing was so beautiful that even the birds listened, and when he played the harp, grown men wept.

Arion was kept busy at King Periander's beck and call. If the King was in a bad temper, Arion was summoned to sing a comic song. If the King was worried by affairs of state, Arion would sing something beautiful to ease his mind. And if the King couldn't sleep, Arion was summoned to sing him a lullaby.

But although Arion was happy at court, he had heard of a great music competition in Sicily and longed to compete.

"Certainly not!" roared Periander. "You could be away for months on end and some other royal court might tempt you away. I won't hear of it!"

Arion was disappointed, and that day his singing lacked sincerity and his playing was dull.

As he lay in bed that night, King Periander thought again about Arion's request. *I suppose if a musician from my court were to win this competition, it would reflect very well on our great city of Corinth and, indeed, on me as a great and cultured king. Maybe I should let Arion go after all.*

So the next morning Arion was summoned to the royal presence and given permission to take part in the festival on the condition he agreed to return to the court of Corinth. Arion promised faithfully.

A few days later, Arion set off for
Sicily on a merchant ship, the cries of
the gulls ringing in a bright blue sky
and the people of Corinth calling their
good wishes as the boat pulled out of
the harbor.

Arion enjoyed the voyage. He loved
the creaking, rolling boat, with its
flapping sails and its cargo of oil and

wine. A fresh wind helped them on their way and before too long they were sailing into the harbor in Sicily. The ship was to wait in port until the competition was over and Arion was ready to return.

He stepped ashore and set off for the festival. It was held in the central square that was festooned with flags and streamers. People flocked to hear musicians from all over the world. There were pipers and poets, flautists and drummers, singers of passionate arias and simple folk tunes. The audience listened, delighted. The festival lasted for three days and three nights and Arion was one of the last to perform.

Everyone was tired by now and so full
of glorious music that there was scarcely
room for more.

But when Arion stepped onto the
stage, something magical happened. As
he struck the first chords on his golden
harp and sang his first clear note, every
living creature, from the wolves on
the hillsides to the cats in the streets,
stopped and listened. The crowd in the
town square held their breath as Arion's
beautiful music wound its way into their
hearts.

It was clear that he had won the
contest. Amid tumultuous applause,
Arion stepped proudly up to the stage
to collect his prize – a bag of gold. The

crowd cheered wildly and showered the hero with petals.

Arion was still on a cloud of happiness the next day when the boat left for Corinth.

"You did all right for yourself, young Arion," said the captain. "I couldn't earn that amount of money if I worked till I was ninety!"

The boat pulled out of the harbor and into open sea, leaving the safety of land behind.

The captain spoke again. "It hardly seems fair, does it lads, that he should make that much gold for a few songs?" The crew were silent, pulling hard on the oars and hauling on the ropes, sweat breaking on their brows as they worked.

Arion began to feel fearful. "It's not
the money that's important to me,"
he stammered. "I love to sing, to give
pleasure to my audience. That is all the
reward I need."

"Not interested in the money?" said
the captain. "Well, you won't mind if we
take it then, will you?"

"No," said Arion. "I care nothing for it!"

"But," continued the captain, "how
will it make us look to our king if you
tell him what has happened? We would
be punished and we can't have that."

"Oh I won't tell the king," said Arion.
"I'll say I lost the gold!"

"I don't believe that," responded the

captain. "It's the first thing you would do. You can't go back to Corinth. The sea is getting rougher – it would be very easy for you to fall overboard ..."

Arion was very frightened now. "If I must die," he cried, "let me play on my harp just one more time, and sing a song to please the gods before I leave this earth ..."

So Arion sat in the prow of the ship and played and sang with all his heart. He sang for the beauty of the ocean, for the blue sky and the bright stars at night. He sang for the soft wind and

the spring rain and the turning of the seasons.

And when he had finished his song, the greedy captain pushed him into the sea, leaving him to drown.

Arion drifted down through the water, deeper under the waves, darkness engulfing him ...

Then, quite suddenly, he was lifted up, rushing toward the light and breaking the surface. He took a great lungful of air – and realized he had been rescued by a dolphin.

The dolphin had been following the ship, enchanted by Arion's singing, and had rushed to save him when he was pushed into the water. Arion wrapped his arms around her smooth gray body with gratitude for being alive! He could feel the dolphin speak to him – "I will take you home," she said, "as long as you sing for me on our journey! Music makes my heart leap and my flippers twitch!"

And so it was that some days later the people of Corinth witnessed the extraordinary sight of Arion, singing at the top of his voice, playing his harp and sitting astride a dolphin, returning triumphantly to the safety of the harbor. They were so excited and proud to hear that he had won the music competition that they bore him up on their shoulders and carried him through the streets to tell King Periander the wonderful news. Great celebrations followed, with drink and festivities and endless congratulations.

Day faded into night and still the

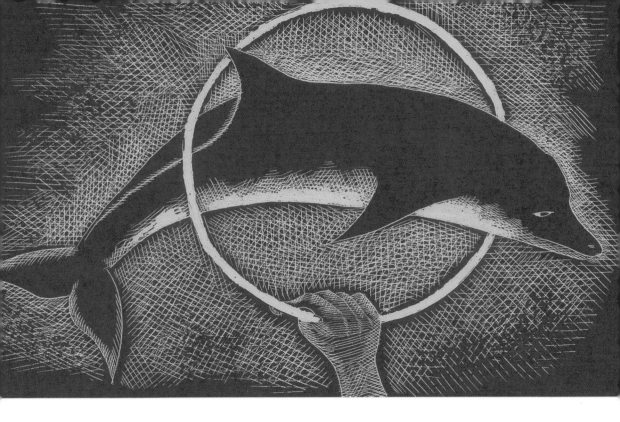

festivities continued. But after a while Arion suddenly thought of the dolphin and wondered where she was. To his horror he found that she had been captured by the fisherfolk and enclosed in a small pool. They were forcing the poor creature to jump through a hoop for dead fish to entertain the crowds.

Arion was furious. "How could you treat this noble creature like that?" he

shouted at the crowd. He hauled the dolphin from the pool, carrying her in his arms to the sea, to release her. But it was too late. He realized that his friend was dying. He knelt, holding her gently, tears spilling down his cheeks. "Forgive me, my friend," he wept. "How have I repaid your kindness to me?"

As Arion knelt, head bowed, holding

the dolphin's dead body, he didn't notice
the ship setting anchor in the harbor
and the captain and crew who had stolen
his gold coming ashore. King Periander,
who had come looking for Arion, was
standing on the quayside and the captain
ran forward and knelt before him.

"Sire," he said, before the king could
speak, "such a dreadful thing happened
on our return voyage. Dear Arion, who
won the music competition, and of
whom we were so proud, was washed
overboard by a freak wave as we left the
port of Sicily. He had the prize money
tied to his belt and the weight of it
caused him to sink beneath the waves
before we could rescue him. Such a loss,

Sire, such grief we felt ..."

King Periander looked confused. "But Arion is here in Corinth – we have been celebrating his triumphant return!" And as he spoke, Arion, tears still wet on his cheeks, stepped forward.

The captain looked shocked and began to stammer an explanation. Arion was full of grief and anger.

"What poor things we humans are!" he shouted. "This captain and his crew, full of greed and envy, stole my gold and left me to drown! And then the people of Corinth, in their ignorance and cruelty, caused the death of the wild creature that showed me compassion and saved my life!

The dolphin had more kindness and appreciation of what is beautiful than any of you!" He strode off, up into the mountains, and sat all night grieving for his lost friend. It was a long time before Arion could play his wonderful music again.

The great god Zeus looked down on the body of the gentle dolphin with great sadness. He took her up and placed her among the stars to commemorate her kindness.

You can still see her
today, a scattering of light
in the darkness of the heavens.

THE KRAKEN

The Kraken, in legend, is a giant sea monster like a huge squid or octopus, with tentacle arms that could wrap around a ship and drag it down into the depths of the ocean. It was so vast that sailors often mistook it for an island, sometimes sailing toward it before realizing too late that they were sailing to their doom. In this poem, the British Poet Laureate (from 1850 till his death in 1892), Alfred, Lord Tennyson, creates an extraordinarily atmospheric picture of a terrifying, brooding presence deep under the ocean.

Below the thunders of the upper deep;

Far, far beneath in the abysmal sea,

His ancient, dreamless, uninvaded sleep

The Kraken sleepeth: faintest sunlights flee

About his shadowy sides: above him swell

Huge sponges of millennial growth
and height;
And far away into the sickly light,
From many a wondrous grot
and secret cell
Unnumbered and enormous polypi
Winnow with giant arms
the slumbering green.

There hath he lain for ages and will lie

Battening upon huge sea-worms in

his sleep,

Until the latter fire shall heat the deep;

Then once by man and angels to be seen,

In roaring he shall rise and on the surface die.

– Alfred, Lord Tennyson

RAVEN AND
THE WHALE

According to the Inuit, it was Raven, with his great glossy wings and his strong beak, who created the world. He was a god, but winged like a bird and with the heart of a man. He worked hard to make the world and to create all the people and animals that fill it. He grew fond of them all and curious as to how things would turn out for them. So, when it was all finished, instead of flying away and thinking of some new grand scheme, he decided to stay on and see what happened ...

Every day Raven paddled out to sea in his kayak to see how everything was doing. One day he saw a huge whale. He remembered making the whale, of course – who could forget – but he couldn't for the life of him remember what it was like on the inside.

So he waited until the whale yawned – an enormous yawn – and he paddled

right in! He secured his kayak to a
huge tooth and set off walking, deeper
and deeper into the dark cavern of
the whale's body. All around him he
could hear the thunderous rhythmic
drumming of the whale's great heart.
White ribs rose up around him like
ivory pillars. Through the gloom, in the
distance, a soft light shone. As Raven
drew closer, he saw that the light was a
lamp, and in the light of the lamp was
a beautiful young girl dancing, swaying
back and forth to the rhythm of the

heartbeat. Attached to her hands and feet were threads stretching out and away to the heart of the whale. When she danced slowly, the whale's heartbeat slowed too, and he floated calmly in the water. When she quickened her pace, the whale plunged and soared through the waves.

The girl smiled at Raven with such gentleness that he fell instantly in love. *I would like to sweep her up in my wings, and fly away and marry her,* he thought.

Out loud
he announced,
"Beautiful girl – I
am Raven and I
made the world.
Come with me,
out into the great
outdoors, and be
my wife."

But the girl
smiled and said,
"I'm afraid I can't
do that because I
am the soul of the
whale, his heart
and his spirit.
But you can stay

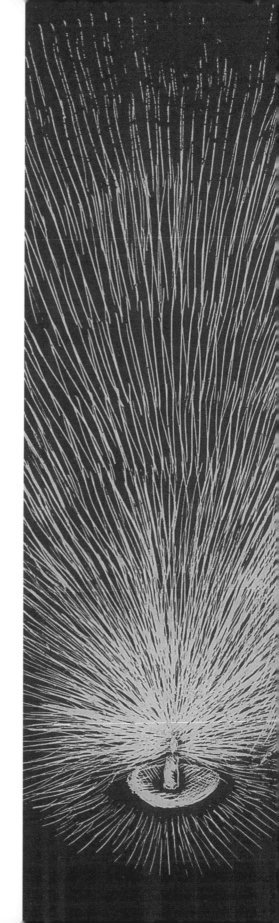

with me here if you like and keep me company."

So Raven flipped back his wings, sat down with his hands on his knees, and watched the girl dance.

Evening came. He felt a breeze ruffle his feathers and looked up. High above him was the whale's spout, and Raven could see through it to the starry sky above. As night came on, the girl's dance became slower and slower, and the whale began to fall asleep.

Suddenly, on impulse, Raven snatched up the sleepy girl and soared away with her, up through the whale's spout and out into the starry night sky. The strings pulled tight and snapped.

Glancing behind him, Raven saw the whale thrashing and plunging in the dark ocean. It was dying. Its huge body was washed up onto the shore where it lay gleaming in the moonlight. In his arms the beautiful girl became smaller and smaller, until she trickled away to nothing.

Raven realized too late that every living creature needs its soul. He was overcome with sorrow at his own foolishness and wept for many days.

But when he had finished his weeping, he began to sing instead, and after that he began to dance. And the tide advanced and receded and the sun rose and fell in the sky and that is how life continued.

THE SEAL WIFE

This is a Selkie story. A Selkie is a sea creature that, like a mermaid, can sometimes come ashore, as long as she keeps hold of her link with home — the Selkie's link is her soft sealskin.

There are many such tales from the wild and lonely Shetland Islands, which lie off the northeast coast of Scotland, where birds and seals outnumber the people and the wind blows across the remote shores. Seals have something of a human look and, like dolphins, they seem to be drawn to people, as curious about us as we are about them.

John Goodman was a handsome young man, tall and broad-shouldered with blue eyes and black hair. As he walked around the island of Orkney, the young women gazed at him, hoping he would notice them.

Beautiful Catriona tried to get him to dance with her at a wedding, but he refused. Morag, quick-witted and full of ideas,

baked him a delicious pie. John ate it but wouldn't speak to her.

Fiona, kind and full of life, gathered a basket of cockles from the seashore. John took them, but shut his door in her face.

John's old mother Annie was worried. "Why don't you take one of these lovely girls for your wife?" she asked. "It's not good for a man to be on his own. I won't be around forever and I'd like to see you settled before I die."

"Mother," said John, "I'm far too busy to be bothered with a wife. I have a farm to run and the seas to fish. Why should I trouble myself with courting?"

Old Annie wept. "Why do you have such a hard heart, my son? I fear for you. One day you will meet a girl who melts your heart, and it will be too late – you will be too old and she won't return your love."

John just laughed. "You worry too much – I'm fine as I am. I don't think

I'll ever fall in love, but if I do I'm sure the girl will love me back. They all do!"

But the young women on the island began to turn against him. "Just who does he think he is?" they muttered, "carrying on as if none of us is good enough for him."

Well, the years rolled by, as the years do. The girls who had once admired him found husbands and had babies. Old Annie died, and John was left alone. His days were filled with farming, and fishing the gray waters around the island. He worked hard and scarcely took time even to lift his head and watch the clouds, or listen to the birds wheeling and swooping above him.

But one evening as he was hauling in his boat, he heard laughter coming from the next cove. Something in the joy of the sound made him stop what he was doing and clamber across the rocks to see who was there.

He crouched down, out of sight, and gazed at the scene before him. A group of people – men, women and children – were playing together on the beach. John had never seen such beautiful, happy people in his life before.

One young girl, in particular, caught his eye. She had long sleek black hair, her skin was as white as a pearl, and her eyes were as dark as a stormy sea. As Annie had predicted so long ago, John

felt his heart melt within him and he
fell deeply in love. Just in front of
him, on top of the rocks he was hiding
behind, there was a pile of silky
sealskins. John realized that he was
looking at Selkie folk, seal people who
can take human form.

John stood up and, immediately, the Selkies saw him and rushed for their skins. But the lovely young woman had been distracted by sea glass in the sand and wasn't as quick as the others. John grabbed the only remaining skin on the rocks and put it in his knapsack. The beautiful girl looked here and there for her skin but it was nowhere to be found. The other seals jumped back into the sea, looking over their shoulders at their sister, stranded and weeping on the shore. They cried long mournful cries in farewell and disappeared beneath the waves.

The poor girl sat on the sand and cried. After a few moments, John approached her.

"Don't be afraid," he said. "I will look after you."

"But I want to go back to the sea, to my family. I don't want to stay here – it's cold and lonely and I have nowhere to go."

"You can come with me," said John. "We will live together in my croft* where it's warm and sheltered."

The poor young girl had no choice. Without her sealskin she was trapped on the land and John Goodman was offering her a home. Weeping, she followed him.

John married the Selkie girl and they lived together in his croft. As time went by she became calmer and grew to love

* Croft – a small stone house with an enclosed area of land for growing food.

him. They had seven children, all of them beautiful, with big dark eyes, sleek black hair and slight webbing between their fingers. And they were all fearless swimmers.

John hid the sealskin under the croft roof, where no one would ever find it.

But he worried when he saw his beloved
wife gazing out to sea with longing in
her eyes. Her moods fluctuated with the
tides. But she loved her children and
was a wonderful wife and mother.

Well, the years rolled by, as the years
will, and the children were growing fast.
One day when the year was turning,
John was away ploughing the top field.
The children were playing around the
croft because the weather was wet and
cold. They started to play hide-and-
seek and the youngest child, a little girl
called Katie, managed to squeeze herself
into the space under the roof. There she
found the soft speckled-gray sealskin,
and it was so warm and comforting that

she pulled it around her and fell asleep, quite forgetting the game going on downstairs.

Some hours later she wandered down to the kitchen still wrapped in the warm skin. Her mother was standing at the fire, stirring a pot of stew, but when she saw Katie she gave a wild cry like nothing the child had ever heard before.

"Where did you find that?" she said, kneeling before the little girl. She took the child in her arms, rocking her and weeping. Katie was puzzled and frightened. She thought she was in trouble for bringing the skin.

The Selkie took the skin and wrapped herself in it. She kissed and held her little daughter, clasping her to her heart. Great tears fell from her dark eyes and she said, "Never doubt that I love you and all your brothers and sisters."

And with that she rushed from the house to the seashore and dived beneath the waves.

John Goodman never saw his Selkie wife again. But sometimes when the children were swimming in the gray waters, a beautiful seal came and swam with them, racing and leaping in the waves.

WHALESONG

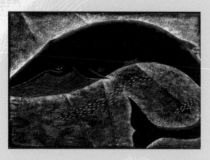

I needed a poem to finish this book, and couldn't find quite the right thing in my collection.

One day I was traveling on the Tube *(the underground train system in London) and happened to glance up – and there it was, printed on a poster in the train car, the perfect poem to end the book. Part of* Poems on the Underground, *an imaginative program that brings poetry to passengers, this poem was the 2010 winner of the* Young Poets on the Underground *competition. It is wonderful to be able to bring it to you here.*

I boom-mumble I bass-blow

I hull-heavy I big/slow

I boat-bump I limpet-skin

I soft-sink I sky-swim

I sea-search I salt-swallow

I bone-backed I fluke-follow

I gulf-cross I listen-talk

I moon-map I wave-walk

I tail-turn I time-keep

I ship-wreck I song-seek

I blue-blood I grumble-sing

I fish-heart I dream king

— Sophie Stephenson-Wright

Acknowledgments
and sources

Story research by Ann Jungman and Jane Ray.

The Kingdom Under the Sea – this story is one of the most popular fairy tales in Japan, and many variations are to be found. I have drawn on one retold by Edmund Dulac (1882–1953), and also **Myths and Legends of Japan** by F.H. Davis (1917).

The Lobster Quadrille – taken from **Alice's Adventures in Wonderland** by Lewis Carroll, England (1832–1898).

The Little Mermaid – my retelling is based on the original story by Hans Christian Andersen, Denmark (1805–1875).

The Fisherman and His Wife – this is a story that appears in different versions the world over, including Russia and China, but I've based my retelling on the Grimm Brothers' (19th century) story in their collection of fairy tales, **The Juniper Tree.**

A Ballad of John Silver – John Masefield, England (1878–1967). Reprinted here by kind permission of The Society of Authors as the Literary Representative of the Estate of John Masefield.

Monkey and Shark – this is a popular African folktale and I've based my version on retellings by Andrew Lang in **The Lilac Fairy Book** (published in 1910) and **East African Folktales** by Vincent Muli Wa Kituku (published in 1997 by August House Inc.).

Arion and the Dolphin – this is a Greek myth, told many times over. I looked at an ancient version by Heroditus who was a Greek researcher and storyteller in the 5th Century BC, and a retelling by the novelist Vikram Seth, published by Orion Books, that I illustrated in 1994.

The Kraken – Alfred, Lord Tennyson, England (1809–1892).

Raven and the Whale – a myth from the Inuit people. I've based my version of the story on retellings by Laura Simms, **Stories that Nourish the Hearts of our Children**, (Holland-Knight Publication 2001) and Ronald Melzak's **Raven – Creator of the World** (published by McClelland and Stewart Ltd. Toronto/Montreal).

The Seal Wife – this is a Selkie story called **The Goodman of Wasteness from the Orkneys.** There are many such tales found in Faroese, Scottish, Icelandic and Hebridean culture. My retelling here is based mainly on a story told by Sigurd Towrie on his website www.orkneyjar.com.

Whalesong – written by Sophie Stephenson-Wright and winner of the Poems on the Underground competition run by the Poetry Society in 2010, which invited science-themed submissions to celebrate the Royal Society's 350th anniversary. Originally printed as part of the Young Poets on the Underground Series.